How To
Love a

Werewolf

How To Love A Werewolf

Sophie Collins

spruce

An Hachette UK Company

First published in Great Britain in 2010 by
Spruce, a division of Octopus Publishing Group Ltd
Endeavour House, 189 Shaftesbury Avenue, London WC2H 8JY
www.octopusbooks.co.uk
www.octopusbooksusa.com

Distributed in the U.S. and Canada for Octopus Books USA
c/- Hachette Book Group USA
237 Park Avenue
New York, NY 10017

Copyright © Octopus Publishing Group Ltd 2010

ISBN 13 978-1-84601-368-3
ISBN 10 1-86401-368-2

A CIP catalogue record of this book is available from the British Library.

Printed and bound in China

10 9 8 7 6 5 4 3 2 1

This book contains the opinions and ideas of the author. It is intended to provide
helpful and informative material on the subjects addressed in this book and is
sold with the understanding that the author and publisher are not engaged in
rendering any kind of personal professional services in this book. The author
and publisher disclaim all responsibility for any liability, loss or risk, personal
or otherwise, that is incurred as a consequence, directly or indirectly, of the
use and application of any of the contents of this book.

Contents

Introduction

Do you fancy a walk on the wild side? No wonder. Werewolves have recently caught up with vampires in the popularity polls as the fun-loving girl's must-have sidekick.

Werewolves aren't just blessed with flowing locks and incredible abs. If you look a bit closer you'll find that a were-boy has some other, even better, qualities: kindness, loyalty, and a real flair for having fun. Plus this furry fella is so protective that if you win his friendship, he'll look after you as carefully as if you were a day-old pup; and he is so warm that you'll hardly ever need a jacket...

So, you're interested, but you need some info before you hook up with a werewolf to make sure that you start off on the right track? You've come to the right place. This is everything you need to know about finding and befriending a were-boy—his favorite hang outs, how to chat to him away from his pack (this guy's almost always part of a tight posse), what his biggest interests are, and, most important of all, why he makes a really awesome friend.

We don't fudge the more challenging side of things, either. You'll also find plenty of advice on what to do when he loses his temper (things can get a bit hairier than with the average teen boy), how to play the pack to your advantage, and how to tell if your new pal is (gulp!) the Alpha of his group. Learn how to run with wolves without upsetting them, how to introduce your own friends into the mix, and what to do if you find yourselves becoming more than just friends.

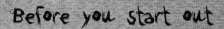

Before you start out

★ You'll need a good torch—werewolves are most active at night.

★ Best to have a taste for the great outdoors, too—were-guys hate hot, crowded places, so be ready to mingle well away from the bright lights.

★ Take a girlfriend or three along. Wolves are happiest in numbers, so you may want your own posse around you.

★ Stay mellow. Were-guys love calm, cheerful girls (they keep the stress levels down). First time out, you want to meet the boy, not the wolf.

   OK, off you go. And happy hunting!

The Wolf Next Door

You've read the books, you've seen the movies—but they don't say much about how to pick a werewolf up once you've tracked him down. The good news is that most werewolves are closer to home than you think. But how do you tell a were-boy from the average hormonally challenged teen fella?

If you fancy your chances of getting close to a werewolf, read on! We'll tell you why a wolf can be a girl's best friend, how to spot him and hit it off, plus plenty of stay-safe tips to help you steer clear of any sudden, umm, changes. So get hunting!

Get Tracking

So how and where can you spot a werewolf? It's a trickier sport than vamp hunting—wolf-boys tend to hang out in packs, just like the regular kind.

Here are some of the likeliest locations:

Extreme sports club

Werewolves love adrenalin—they can't get enough of that high-risk buzz. If you're into action yourself, try out snowboarding, abseiling, or high-diving, and look for the guy taking it all in his (huge) stride. If you're less keen on racking your own nerves, watch from the sidelines: You'll be able to keep a sharp eye out for potential wolf posses.

Favorite diner

Think of your average boy's humungous appetite. Now double it. Teen werewolves are putting on muscle faster than a gym-bound beefcake, and they're *really* hungry, all the time. Sign up for some after-school waitressing at the most popular local burger joint, and watch out for the hungriest hotties.

Survival course

If you're hoping to hang with wolves, then honing your wilderness skills is sensible. But your average wolf-boy needs to learn about the great outdoors too—after all, he's going to be spending plenty of time in the woods. Sign up for a course and partner yourself with the fella who just exudes animal magnetism.

In the garage

Maybe you don't love cars and bikes, but if you want a werewolf pal, you'll learn to feign an interest. Were-boys are born grease monkeys; they're fantastic at fixing any kind of machine. Plus this is one place where you're unlikely to be fighting off much female competition to catch his eye.

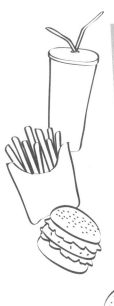

No-go for Wolves

Werewolves hate crowds and their internal thermostats are sent spiralling by too much heat. They aren't known for their cultural leanings either. Museums, art galleries, and any high-school dance or disco all tend to be wolf-free zones.

Quiz: Where's Wolfy?

Is that the real call of the wild you're hearing? Find out if you've learned enough to pick your furry fella from the regular pack.

---

1 No doubt he's cute, but what first caught your eye?

a. His buff bod. He's got abs to die for. ☆

b. His thick, glossy hair. I'm jealous! ☆

c. His geek chic. Nerdy glasses and a buttoned-up shirt somehow look good on him. ☆

d. His natural style, whatever he's doing. ☆

---

2 You shared study night and snuck a peek in his bathroom. What did you find?

a. Soap, towel, razor. Really basic. ☆

b. Haircare central—he uses three types of conditioner. ☆

c. A stack of books by the bath and a rubber ducky. Cute! ☆☆

d. A huge tub, gilt taps…this guy knows how to live! ☆

---

3 Where are you most likely to run into him?

a. At the skatepark with his mates.
b. At the gym, working out.
c. At the library, catching up with schoolwork.
d. At the mall, scoping out the latest designer lines.

4 You meet in town. How does he greet you?

a. With a big grin and a high five. He's delighted to see you.
b. Friendly but casual: "Hi, how're things?"
c. He stammers and blushes like crazy…awww!
d. Smooth and charming—he's always got a line ready.

5 He's been put in charge of your class's term trip. What does he pick?

a. An evening's go karting—fun for the whole gang.
b. A day's paintballing, so he can show off his perfect aim.
c. A museum trip, with extra notes he wrote himself.
d. A night stargazing somewhere close to the wild.

6 You're planning a day in the country with your friends. Which do you think he'd prefer?

a. A hike in the woods, then a big campfire barbecue.
b. A few hours climbing rocks at an outdoor adventure center.
c. A birdspotting outing, complete with guide and binoculars.
d. A trip to a wildlife park. He really loves big cats.

Answers: Where's Wolfy?

Mostly As
Congratulations—you've done your homework and this guy is probably the real deal. He's active, he's super-toned, he loves to hang out in a gang, he's got no time for fakers, and he's naturally *really* warm. All true signs of a werewolf, 21st-century style.

Mostly Bs
We can see why you thought this boy might run with the pack, but appearances are deceptive. Real werewolves don't hit the gym (they don't have to), and they're not too interested in grooming, either. Hair products and work outs? Sounds more like a fella who's into himself than a team player with a wild side.

The Real Deal

Gym Bunny

Mostly Cs

Girl! What are you thinking? This guy will clearly be a sweet study buddy when you're having trouble with homework, and his culture-vulture qualities would make him a great gallery buddy. You shouldn't need telling, though, that despite the pleading puppy-dog eyes, he's no kind of wolf.

Mostly Ds

Hmm...very, very cool? With a taste for big game, and perfect personal style? This guy is giving out non-human vibes, but they don't say were-boy. Are you absolutely sure this one isn't fanged rather than furry? Because he sounds an awful lot like a vampire.

Boy Genius

Fanged Fella

Common Myths

There's plenty of musty lore and legend on werewolves—but which bits should you take on board? Look up "werewolf" online and you'll find a mash-up between sensitive lost soul and something out of a horror movie. Don't believe all you read, though—here are some of those myths debunked (plus a few with a grain of truth).

Werewolf lore

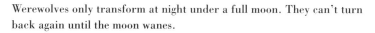

Moon madness

Werewolves only transform at night under a full moon. They can't turn back again until the moon wanes.

True or false? Huh? Maybe this was true in some distant land of long ago and far away, but your modern werewolf has family, school, and a love life to juggle. He can't be running around at the beck and call of a big rock in the sky. False.

Temper, temper

Don't upset a werewolf when he's in human form—if he gets emotional, he won't be able to help transforming.

True or false? There's some truth here. Young werewolves who are just getting used to "turning wolf" take time to get themselves under control. For the first year or two, if you excite or anger one he may take on his furry form unexpectedly. It's just one step on from your average teenage tantrum.

Hot spots

You'll know a werewolf because he feels hot to the touch. Boiling blood runs through his veins.

True or false? Hmm. Partly true. A were-boy's blood doesn't boil exactly, but his body temperature is the same as that of a wolf—and that's several degrees higher than the average human. Of course this makes him a hot date for those cold winter evenings; you can leave the extra scarf at home.

Faux fur

You can tell a werewolf in human shape by the fur growing on the palms of his hands.

True or false? Eww, gross. This fur rumor is definitely false. Apart from just a few seconds mid-change, were-boys are either 100 percent human or 100 percent wolf: no half-measures in the shapeshifter world.

Sterling shot

You can only kill a werewolf with a silver bullet.

True or false? Silver bullets are just like any other kind—they could do some damage, but only if you had enough of them (and who's got that much spare bling lying about?). And it's not the only thing that they're in danger from—jealous vamp-boys can be pretty deadly to a werewolf too.

Teenage Kicks

You've seen it in a hundred movies: that menacing moment when boy morphs into wolf. But what's it like in real life? Should you scream? Run? Give him a calming pat on the head? Here's what to do when "The Rage Issue" crops up.

"You wouldn't like me when I'm angry…"

Boys! One moment you're having a heated discussion about what band to see on Saturday night…the next he's started shaking all over—and within seconds, you're sharing the room with a super-scary wolf and a pile of shredded boy-clothes. Stay cool and remember that in wolf world a sudden phasing—that's were-speak for transforming—is just your average teen tantrum. He's probably more scared than you are.

Here's the 5-step plan to remember when your favourite fella turns furry:

(1) **Keep still.** There's often a bit of thrashing about during the change, and you don't want to catch a flying paw (or claw). He's not likely to hurt you on purpose, so make it your aim to avoid accidents.

(2) **Be calm.** Your wolf-boy can't speak English when he's in animal mode, but he'll understand you, and you'll find it surprisingly easy to read his lupine looks.

(3) **Let him out.** Most werewolves want to get outdoors into moonlight when they're in wolf form. Let him go—you can trot alongside (or hop on for a ride!) to keep him company. Or you could just stay in the warm and see him in class.

(4) **Be polite.** Don't be rude about his shapeshifting status. Werewolves are proud of their history and heritage, so don't laugh at him or talk disrespectfully about his wolf side.

(5) **Don't be nosy.** Above all, don't play 20 Questions when he's back in his boy body. If the change is a little scary to watch, just think how it must feel to do. Wait for him to bring the subject up and be ready with a shoulder to cry on if he wants to tell you about the downsides.

When things get back to normal, reassure yourself that there's no harm done, and remember not to get his hackles up next time!

Boy in Wolf's Clothing

Girls fresh to the wereworld often ask if they'd be able to tell their transformed pal from the rest of the pack—and the answer is yes, if you know what to look for. It's not all about a cold nose and a shiny coat! Your wolf-boy's key qualities don't change, even when his species does.

Use this chart to find your four-legged friend.

Breed of Boy	Which Wolf?
* The gentle, sensitive type, who tends to calm things down rather than rev them up. Undoubtedly the peacemaker of the group.	* Look for a full face and round, large eyes, a short, silky-soft coat, and a smooth run that's maybe not so fast as the other wolves'.
* A natural No. 1, this is the kind of guy all the others listen to. He definitely sets the pace, and the rest of the group fall into line.	* Need you ask? Even as a boy, he's head of the pack; as a wolf, he's the huge Alpha out front, with the brightest eyes and the loudest howl.
* The get-things-done-guy, who stands out even among a bunch of can-do were-boys. There's no problem so big this boy can't fix it.	* He's a practical dark brown, with big, pointy ears and a keen, alert look. The pack scout, he'll act as lookout for any hunters (or vampires!).
* The class clown who's always goofing around and who sees life as one long joke. He's up for a laugh and loves playing pranks on people.	* The joker of the pack. Small and quick, this wolf's as playful as a cub with his packmates. Ever seen a wolf smile? This one never stops.

THE VERDICT?
Did you recognize your human pal in this lupine lineup?

What's His Type?

There aren't many true wolf-girls about, but there's plenty about the normal kind for a werewolf to love. Uncover his turn-ons (and a few turn-offs) with this checklist.

Keep it natural

Most boys love genuine girls, and your furry fella is no exception. Easy manners and plenty of natural chat will encourage him to let his guard down and be himself with you. What he hates? Over-the-top flirting, bitchy gossip, and insincerity. He may have transformation issues of his own, but there's nothing tricky about this boy—he prefers his friends to be open and honest.

Get outdoors

Werewolves can't bear to be confined. A love of the great outdoors can only strengthen your appeal; add a shot of action-girl adrenalin and you'll become irresistible. White-water rafting, free climbing, or off-piste snowboarding will all appeal to an energetic wereboy. If that sounds a bit heavy-duty, start at the shallow end and try a cycle ride or a short hike. You never know, you might get a taste for the outdoors.

Run with the pack

Loyalty's a huge issue with werewolves and they like a team player. The early horror movies got it all wrong. Far from being antisocial loners, they're most comfortable in a group, and are happiest looking out for one another. Make it clear that you're a keeper: You take good care of your friends and you expect them to do the same for you. He'll love you for it.

Stay grounded

Despite the shapeshifting, werewolves are down-to-earth types who don't have much time for emotional games. Uber-fit and grounded themselves, they like self-sufficient people who can pull their weight. Drama queens need not apply! If you scream the place down when you break a nail and you always have to summon help when there's a spider in the tub, are you sure you want to run with wolves?

THE VERDICT?
Active, loyal, fun-loving, and practical? If you ticked all the boxes, congratulations—you're a natural were-pal.

Good Wolf, Bad Wolf

So, does he dig his wolf powers, or would he sooner be all boy? Take a wolf's-eye look at the pros and cons of being a shapeshifter—what's cool and what's not.

It's cool...

* Being faster, fitter, and stronger than a regular guy—almost like having superpowers.

* Acting on instinct without worrying about manners.

* Having a secret that's shared only with the rest of the pack.

* Impressing girls.

* Scaring off vampires.

* Feeling so close to the natural world.

But it sucks...

* Phasing with no warning when things suddenly get emotional. Every teen loses his temper!

* When you rip up your favorite jeans every time.

* Having to keep secrets from your friends and family, for their own good.

* Freaking girls out.

* A blood feud...at this age?

* Scaring so many wild creatures...and pets!

THE VERDICT?

It turns out that wolves have a gentle side. Do you want to learn more? Or will he drive you wild with worry?

Wolf Talk

You've met, there's a good vibe, and when you chat you feel there's a connection—but can you talk to him about anything, or are some subjects out of bounds? Under the skin most werewolves are sensitive souls, so make sure you pick the right topics—you don't want fur to fly!

Check out our foolproof guide to the savviest were-proof subjects.

Bring up

★ **Track sports.** Plenty of were-boys excel on the track even when they're in human form. And once these guys switch to four feet, they're the fastest things on earth (not many other species can outrun a vampire…). He can talk top speeds, technique, plus a few digs at the "competition" for hours. Don't bring it up unless you're a *really* good listener.

★ **Haircare.** You might want to be subtle about this one, but most new werewolves are pretty pleased with their pelts. Boys who were never into the latest cuts may suddenly start displaying an interest in conditioner. Help him out with the lowdown on your favorite brands.

★ **Fashion.** He doesn't look like a label-loving clotheshorse, but he needs new clothes and plenty of them (and with his muscles, you're talking big sizes). Talk through his cheap'n'chic options and enjoy teaching him something about style—it's bad enough that his outfits get ripped to bits whenever he changes; it's even worse when they weren't worth saving in the first place!

Keep off

★ **Anger management.** Even if you feel he could use the reminder, steer clear of advice on this topic. He's all too aware of what happens if he blows a fuse, and won't appreciate your special deep-breathing routines, even if you're just trying to help.

★ **Vampires.** Werewolves and vamps don't get along. Period. But age-old blood feuds aren't something to discuss in polite wolf company, so if you want things to stay fun, steer clear of the V-word altogether.

★ **Dog training.** It's an easy mistake to make. After all, he knows all about animal instincts, and your pet pooch needs some training—what could be more natural than to ask for some tips? Wolves absolutely loathe being compared with domestic dogs, so this is a bad blooper. Avoid.

The Wolf Diaries

You went hunting for a werewolf and found a friend. But are you BWB (Best Wolf Buddies) or still at paw's length? Use these pages to chart your friendship ups and downs, and keep an eye on what rubs his fur up the wrong way.

Where we met

....

....

....

....

What I noticed

....

....

....

....

Why he's great to hang out with

....

....

....

....

....

Why he sometimes makes me nervous

....

....

....

....

....

What drives him barking mad

....

....

....

....

....

Walkies and Talkies

So, after ID'ing your were-boy and his pack, being friends is the easy bit, right? Nuh-uh! Werewolves aren't mean, but they're moody (try having not one, but two sets of adolescent hormones howling around inside you!), so be prepared to share some ups and downs, plus some outright ominous silences.

The good part is that as you get to know one another better, you'll find he's the best "friend-who's-a-boy" ever! You'll have fun together, but he'll look out for you, too. Things to do and places to go? Read on...

Must-See Movies

So you're going to hang out for the evening and watch DVDs together? Great idea—and if you want to make him howl with laughter, try choosing a werewolf movie (he'll be able to fill you in on the bits they got wrong). But which one?

Here are our top picks:

1 New Moon (2009)

If you were disappointed at the vamp-heavy content of the first *Twilight* movie, *New Moon* more than makes up for it. The werewolves are cool (and accurate) and there are still two more movies in the series to look forward to—both of them with plenty of wolf action.

2 I Was a Teenage Werewolf (1957)

A cult classic starring a hot-to-trot '50s honey. Loads of errors but cool clothes—and look out for the fabulous original poster on the DVD box.

3 The Curse of the Werewolf (1961)

OK, it's an oldie, but it's got surprisingly good transformation scenes, it's accurate in parts, and it has a nice, straightforward plot.

4 The Wolf Man (1941)

One of the earliest werewolf movies—hilariously hammy acting and loads of snarls from a guy in what looks like a gorilla suit. It's got a fantastic sinister backing track and plenty of swirling fog, too.

5 Wolf (1994)

Jack Nicholson's old enough to be your grandfather, but this is still a fab story with lots of laughs. It's good on some of the super-skills (like an extra-strong sense of smell) that werewolves really *do* have, too.

6 Teen Wolf (1987)

Silly, camp comedy, played for laughs with a sports-mad teen hero. Plus there's plenty of high '80s fashion to enjoy.

7 Van Helsing (2004)

Set in Dracula's original stamping ground, Transylvania, but it's got a wolf-centric-subplot with some seriously awesome transformation scenes. This one's scary enough to watch from behind the sofa!

8 Blood and Chocolate (2007)

If *Twilight* wasn't enough, here's a beautifully shot story with a were-girl at the heart of a doomed love triangle. A bit gory for the faint-hearted, but so many werewolves that you'll be spoilt for choice.

9 An American Werewolf in London (1981)

Another classic—it may be long in the tooth, but this one will still raise the hairs on the back of your neck. Watch with the lights on!

10 The Company of Wolves (1984)

More like a series of fairy stories than a werewolf tale, but it's lovely to look at, and will give you plenty to talk about afterwards.

Time Together

He's not exactly a loner, but the only crowds he really appreciates are groups of his own kind...so when you want to get out and about with your were-boy, where's a good choice (and what's better avoided)?

Hang-out hotspots

Ice skating

The temperature will help him keep his cool, while you can use his radiating body heat to keep *you* warm. Plus, with his terrific balance and turn of speed he'll be a natural out on the ice—and if you're a little shaky, he'll be more than happy for you to cling on to him. Sign up for your local rink and get those skates on!

Surfing

At the other end of the sports spectrum, the same werewolf qualities work just as well on a board. In fact, while you wouldn't ever call a were-boy a jock (he's too cool and independent for that), he'll excel at most sports. You can leave him to show off with his mates while you soak up some sun, or you can join him and hit the surf together.

Stock car racing

Standing alongside the track may not be your idea of a great day out— it's loud, it's dirty, and the cars are wrecks—but if you want to treat him, this should be a hit, with plenty of pace and excitement to rev him up. Think of it as bumper cars for grown-ups, and pack a picnic for two.

Steakhouse

A guy's gotta eat—a wolf's gotta eat *more*. He's always hungry, and while you might pick sushi, this boy will choose meat every time, and lots of it. Save the gourmet cuisine for a girls' night out and let him satisfy his wolf-sized appetite. Remember, steak'n'salad is one of the healthiest choices for you, too.

Football game

Of course, it could be basketball, softball, or any other team game; werewolves love watching teamwork in action, on the pitch or the court. Pick to suit your preference, get in the hot dogs, and settle down to spectate together.

Mini-marathon training

If you've broken every "get fit" resolution you've ever made, it's time to reverse the trend. Werewolves love to run more than almost anything else on earth, so enlist him as coach. Your training will come on in leaps and bounds. Just don't challenge him to a race.

Time Together II

Hang-out howlers

Health club sauna

Given that he loves sports, a sauna session may sound like a great way to recharge after an energetic work out. But don't even think about it. All that steamy heat will warm your buddy beyond his comfort zone, and he may turn unexpectedly furry very fast.

School dance

It's a pity, because he's got a great sense of rhythm and you'd love to share a night on the dance floor, but if you want to strut your stuff you'll need to find somewhere you can do it out of doors. Any sense of confinement stresses a werewolf, and if he gets overheated—well, you won't like him when he's tense... Plus he'd ruin his tux.

Nature trail

He loves roaming the woods, so a lesson on how to follow animal tracks seems a good fit. But animals and birds can smell the wolf vibe a mile off, so you won't spot anything while he's around. Your guy already knows everything he needs to about tracking, so save this one to share with a green-fingered girlfriend.

Yoga class

You find it cool and relaxing, and you thought it might bring out your were-guy's more sensitive side. Plus a werewolf's gotta be pretty flexible. Think again. Were-boys aren't any keener on Lycra and meditation than regular guys. Accept it—he might be a supernatural creature, but some things are just *too* out there, even for him.

Karaoke

You and your girlfriends are killer at karaoke—even if your renditions are a little out of tune, you gals know how to put on a performance. Given that he likes to hang with a gang, a karaoke evening could bring you all together, right? Wrong! One not-so-well-known fact about werewolves is that they have trouble holding a tune. And when they sing together—well, it sounds a lot like a howling chorus.

Thrill Seekers

Even if phasing's the ultimate rush, you don't want to spend all your buddy time with a beast. Luckily, there are plenty of adrenalin highs you can both enjoy together (maybe even for charity), if you've got the nerve to see them through...

How brave are you feeling? Tick off the hair-raising options you think you could handle.

Climbing wall   *Fear Factor: 1/5*

Hmm. Well, it's not the most dangerous choice, but most outdoor centers have a climbing wall with a few optional routes to the top. You can work as a team, which will help to build your trust in one another, and it'll still be a thrill when you reach the top.

High diving   *Fear Factor: 2/5*

Bella swore off cliff diving, and so should you —you want rush, not risk. But the high board at the pool can offer a fantastic swoop before you hit the water. Give it a try. Most werewolves are water babies at heart, so your guy should be happy to come along for the dive.

White-water rafting — *Fear Factor: 3/5*

Now you're talking! White water rafting is bumpy, unpredictable, and fast, with more than a hint of peril. His combination of speed and strength makes your guy the perfect partner for the trip.

Bungee jumping — *Fear Factor: 4/5*

Many people have considered a bungee jump from time to time—and most have thought better of it. But it offers a serious rush with relatively little risk, you'll impress all your friends, and your were-boy will love it—after all, however fast he can run, he can't actually fly.

Parachute jump — *Fear Factor: 5/5*

Jumping out of a plane attached to just a bundle of nylon sheet and some strings... Of course you've got to want to do it, but if you've found yourself wishing for a shapeshifter sized thrill, one jump should answer your thrill-seeking needs for, ooh, at least a week.

THE VERDICT?

Did you have the time (or the fright?) of your life? Remember, it's never worth scaring yourself just to impress someone else, so sit out anything you don't feel comfortable with.

Sharing Secrets

As your friendship grows it'll seem natural for you to want to fill in the gaps with your werewolf pal. When you're a Y-chromosome short, even regular boys can be tough to read; add a dash of wolf and it's even harder to get under his skin (or fur). Boys run a mile from talking about their feelings (and this guy's fast)—so, since he's plenty interested in you too, why don't you take turns asking whatever you want, and promise to answer honestly.

Better get ready to share some secrets!

You could ask him...

* Does he have any "brothers" (wolf or human)?

* How does phasing actually feel? Does it hurt?

* Is he the same inside when he turns furry?

* How did he feel when he found out what he was?

* As a wolf, does he have super-senses?

* Does he know any werewolf girls? Does he like them?

* What's the best thing about being on four feet?

* Does he ever bite, you know, *people*?

He might ask you...

* 98.6°? What's it like being so cold all the time?

* Would *you* ever want the chance to change form?

* Can't you sometimes read your friends' minds, too?

* What do you talk about for all those hours on the phone with your girlfriends?

* Just what is it with girls and *shopping*? (That's a mystery to *all* boys!)

* Do you feel vulnerable without super-powers?

* Does a were-boy stand the same chance with a girl as a regular guy...or a vampire?

WELL?
Were there any big surprises? Do you feel closer now you know more about each other?

Quiz: Time out

Things were going so well—you thought you'd found a boy you could have fun with *and* confide in. But suddenly he's giving you the cold shoulder: "CU l8r?" gets no reply. Is it something you did? Has he called time on you? Or is it just a temporary off-with-the-pack wolf thing? Answer these questions to find out if you're in the doghouse...and why.

1 What does he do when you bump into his pack?
a. Introduces you around; he's keen for you all to get along. ☆
b. Says "Hi," but then hurries on to keep you to himself. ☆
c. Starts goofing around with them—high-fives and in-jokes ☆
only they'd understand.
d. Says "Bye" to you, and goes off with them. ☆

2 He's never exactly chatty, but now he's as silent as the grave. How do you get his tail wagging again?
a. Organize a cool day out, including both your friends. ☆
b. Let him know that you're there if he needs you. ☆
c. Check in with one of his packmates and ask for suggestions. ☆
d. Ignore him until he's stopped sulking. ☆

3 How much have you talked about his furry alter-ego?

a· Plenty. He trusts you enough to open up. ☆

b· Some, but he's always been a little shy about filling you in ☆
on all the furry details.

c· Not too much. He's intensely private. ☆

d· Hardly at all. A free spirit won't explain himself to anyone. ☆

4 Are you ever frightened by his darker moods?

a· Nah. Everyone has mood swings, right? ☆

b· You can take most tantrums in your stride, but sometimes ☆
when his eyes flash yellow you get a tiny bit twitchy.

c· Yes! You've told him that he needs to get a grip. ☆

d· You don't stick around to see them. Better safe than sorry. ☆

5 What was he talking about before he went AWOL?

a· His awesome upcoming month off with his pack. ☆

b· School stuff. But he was acting edgy. ☆

c· He was being mysterious (and totally annoying) about his ☆
packed schedule.

d· Can't remember. You weren't really listening... ☆

6 How does he act when he reappears?

a· He picks right up where he left off. ☆

b· He'll drop hints and scraps about what he's been up to, ☆
but concentrates on what *you've* been doing.

c· He seems uneasy at first, and won't answer your questions. ☆

d· He brushes off any questions; he's here now, isn't he? ☆

Answers: Time Out

Mostly As

Well done! You've won his trust and he can confide in you about his activities as both boy and wolf. He's happy for you to mix with his friends, whether they've got two feet or four paws, and he knows you've got his best interests at heart. Even if he's disappeared to run with the pack, he'll be back in your orbit before too long.

Mostly Bs

It's a solid friendship, and you care about one another's feelings, but he's not sure what you think about his shapeshifting status (and nor are you—you like him, but you're not certain you want to be pals with the whole pack). You could both open up a bit more; you get on so well that it's worth working through your issues together.

Mostly Cs

Hmmm—you're pals, sure, but he's not sure how close. He's scared to open up to you about his, er, "hairier moments" and you're not so sure you want to know either, so he's sheltering you from the gory details. Real friends accept each other, fur and all, so you'll have to make some compromises if you want to make this work.

Mostly Ds

In the words of the (really) old song—you get along without him very well. And it's mutual. Both of you do what you want and neither of you is big on sharing, so right now you're more Facebook friends than soulmates. Fine, if that's all you want. If not, you're going to have to show him he can trust you before he'll open up.

Don't Go Changing

All were-boys start out new to phasing, and for a while it can
be tough for them to control themselves. If your boy gets too
stressed, or even too happy, he'll turn furry whether he wants
to or not, and it can be really sudden (and embarrassing!). He
hates not being in charge of his own body, so how can you
help him hold the hair in check?

Here are some ideas you can try together:

Tai chi

Those slow-mo martial arts classes that you sometimes see in the park on
a summer's day? They may look a bit theatrical, but tai chi is fabulous
for helping you manage both mind and body. It's all about control, not
aggression. He'll certainly find it useful when he feels like he's about to
explode—and it's great for all-round health and well-being, not to
mention toned thighs, so you might as well join in, too.

Mind over matter

Meditation's a time-honoured method that plenty of adult werewolves
use to chill out when things are getting overheated. Whichever technique
you choose, all work on focus and concentration. Were-guys aren't
known for their patience, so it's best to start with a practical, results-
based method that doesn't have too much theory to absorb. Check out
the local options online.

Phase to order

It sounds odd, but if your pal can learn to turn wolf when he wants to, he'll find it easier *not* to turn when he needs to stay boy-shaped. Take a stopwatch and a friend with nerves of steel (that's you!) and get him to change in a set time, against a slow countdown. Make sure you go somewhere private to practice, though; if you try it in your local park, you'll soon have an audience!

Find a mentor

If all methods fail and the smallest stress is still a trigger for turning wolf, he needs a mentor. This is where you stand back—only an experienced werewolf will be able to show him the ropes and teach him how to cope. Older guys in the pack can also reassure him it won't always be this way; it's a rite of passage, and one that plenty of boys would pick over other teen angst factors.

Is She Fur Real?

It's been a hot topic (in more ways than one) in shapeshifting lore for centuries. Are werewolves always guys, or are there were-girls running with the pack, too? You'll find plenty of sources saying different things, so it's time to set the record straight: They're a rare breed, but yes, they do exist!

So what do you need to know about she-wolves?

Making friends

Will she like you? She may, but take it slowly and don't be pushy; she'll probably be more guarded than your average all-girl gang. Like her fellow werewolves, she hates anything insincere or fake, so be open and frank with her and she should warm to you.

Her look

Just as your were-boy is tall, buff, and handsome, the typical were-girl is a Glamazon who's never heard of a bad hair day, with a truly toned bod that's never been inside a gym. Sickening! Personality-wise, most wolf-girls are warm, loyal, and generous, just like their brothers, but this is still one girl you never, ever want to have a serious scrap with.

Biology 101

Ignore the movies. You don't become a werewolf through bites (frankly, if you've annoyed a werewolf to the point of attack, you'll be lucky to survive). The were-factor is in the genes and, put simply, more usually a boy thing. But now and then it crops up in girls, especially when there are vamps around, so don't be surprised if your local pack goes co-ed.

Girl talk

She-wolves are so rare that they're not used to hanging out with other girls who understand their condition, so ask your boy to introduce you and keep your chats general to start with. Music, school stuff, and clothes (she has the same problem as were-boys with phasing, so she goes clothes shopping a lot) should all be safe bets. Don't let her gorgeousness intimidate you either—she has all the same teen issues as you. It's just that her time of the month is *much* more dramatic.

Don't be nosy

Were-girls have a big secret to protect, and can be even more guarded about their privacy than the boys in the pack. Don't bombard her with questions about what it's like to wear a real fur coat and run faster than any human. If she wants to, she'll tell you in her own good time. And if she doesn't, well, you definitely don't want to wind her up.

The Friendship Stakes

You may have been drawn by the novelty originally, but you've learned a lot since then, so if you're picking a BMF (that's best male friend), which is the better bet in the long term: your regular teenage guy, or the one who runs with wolves? It's time to take stock.

Boy Next Door

Pros

* He's easy to read.

* He's laid-back and doesn't easily lose his cool.

* You've known him forever; he's safe and familiar.

* You're into the same books, bands, and movies.

* Sometimes it feels great to hang out with someone who's just ordinary…

Cons

* He's *too* easy to read.

* Happy is good, but he can be a bit predictable.

* You wish that, just once, he'd surprise you.

* He can be a bit slow to try anything new.

* … and sometimes, being with somebody ordinary is just boring.

Boy Wonder

Wolf-Boy

Were-boy Next Door

Pros

* He's got a warm personality and a (literally) hot bod!

* He's always on the go; he has endless energy.

* You find his wolf side incredibly exciting.

* He can fix anything—he even managed to mend your iPod.

* He really understands what close friendship is.

Cons

* Though he tries hard, the moods can be awful.

* Sometimes you wish he'd slow down a bit.

* The sudden phasing can be a bit disconcerting.

* He's not much into culture: galleries and the theatre are off the menu.

* You feel the pack will always come first.

THE VERDICT?

What's your taste in boys (or wolves)? Is there room in your life for both?

The Wolf Diaries II

It's how it usually goes: The closer you get to a friend, the more you learn about both their good and bad sides. Not only has your were-guy taught you a lot about boys (and wolves!), but he's learning a lot from you about how girls behave and feel. You have good times when you're together, but what about when you're with your gang and he's with his pack? Will the picture change? And where's next for you both?

What I've learned

....

....

....

....

What I think I've taught him about girls

....

....

....

....

....

Great things about our friendship

....

....

....

....

Not-so-great things we should discuss

....

....

....

....

Where I see our friendship going from here

....

....

....

....

....

3

Running with the Pack

If you were looking for a friend in the singular, you picked the wrong guy. Like it or loathe it, your were-boy comes as part of a pack, and you'll be seeing a lot of all of them.

So what should you do when you want to get your friend on his own for a bit of one-on-one time? And how can you fix it when your own gang and his pack don't really get along like one big happy family? This section will give you plenty of advice on what to do when things get hairy.

Pack Politics

"His business is our business." It might sound like a line from a cheesy Mafia movie, but this is the dynamic your new best friend lives by. So how exactly does it work?

Be prepared with this guide to cracking pack habits:

All for one

Were-boys look after one another, and not only when they're in a fight. His pack mates will be looking after his emotional interests, too—which includes checking out his non-were friends. This means you. Be ready for every member of the pack to take a friendly interest.

No holds barred

It's tough understanding boundaries when you can read minds, so privacy's just not a pack-friendly concept. Your wolf-boy can't help sharing stuff with his mates, so don't get huffy with him. If he cares about you, they will too. Have a quiet word with him, explaining that you'd prefer that some of your more private chats don't become public discussions. They'll *all* soon get the message.

Hungry hordes

Werewolves travel en-masse, which means that as soon as one drops in, they'll soon have filled your house, emptied your fridge, and then moved on. A visit from the posse can feel as though a plague of locusts has passed by. Stock up on chips and dip.

When fur flies

"Argument" is probably too grand a word: Were-boys shout and squabble like a litter of wolf cubs. So far, so teenage—but most guys don't phase mid-bicker so they can resolve things physically. Having a lounge full of outsized snapping wolves can be hard on the furnishings (your mother definitely wouldn't approve), so raise your voice and tell them to take it outside.

Keeping pace

It's hard to explain just how much energy these guys have. They're constantly active and it can be tiring keeping up. Don't feel you have to try. Their energy levels are superhuman and you fall strictly in the human category. Even if they love having you around (and a cute girl can easily become a pack mascot), feel free to take a few days out whenever you need to. No need to always follow the pack.

Quiz: Are You Part of a Pack?

You've proved that you can cope with a wolf posse, but what about your own gang or clique? OK, you don't head off to howl at the moon or go chasing through the woods together, but it's likely that you and your friends are still a part of some kind of pack. Answer these questions to find out if you're a natural people person, or more of a free spirit.

1 How do you get to know the cute new guy in class?
a. Safety in numbers! You and the girls spend all morning discussing him, before deciding to go sit with him at lunch. ☆
b. Take your best friend for backup and go say "Hey." ☆
c. Catch him on his own and offer to show him around. ☆
d. Do nothing. It's up to him to make the first move. ☆

2 What's your preferred night in?
a. A sleepover: face packs, DVDs, snacks, and girly gossip. ☆
b. A chilled-out chat with a couple of good friends. ☆
c. Alone with your phone. After all, you can talk to anyone you want, but keep them at arm's length. ☆
d. Curled up with a book. Who needs people? ☆

3 Your werewolf guy suggests a night out with the pack. What do you do?

a. Suggest you bring some girls to even up the numbers. ☆

b. Ask if you can bring a friend to dilute the wolf vibe. ☆

c. Agree enthusiastically. All that male attention to yourself! ☆

d. You love his friends, but how about some one-on-one time? ☆

4 What's your ideal birthday outing?

a. A packed gig with your favorite band, and as many people as you can collect. The more the merrier. ☆

b. A beach visit and picnic with your very best friends. ☆

c. Two or three close pals and the new *Twilight* premiere. ☆

d. A long bike ride in the country with whoever wants in. ☆

5 There are a couple of new girls in class; they seem shy and they don't know many people. What do you do?

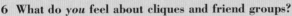

a. Chat to them a bit to see if they'd fit in with your group. ☆

b. Ask them to hang out with you and your friends. ☆

c. Take some time to get to know them. ☆

d. Nothing special. You're sure they'll settle in soon. ☆

6 What do *you* feel about cliques and friend groups?

a. Essential—how else do you feel like you belong somewhere? ☆

b. A mixed blessing. They're great support, but can be intimidating if you're left out of the loop. ☆

c. You don't worry about them and get along with everyone. ☆

d. You'd rather be on your own than follow the crowd. ☆

Answers: Are You Part of a Pack?

Mostly As
You're a true pack animal. You like to do things in a group, and hate being on your own, so you'll absolutely understand how a wolf pack works, too. It's great to feel popular, but make sure you don't fall too much into the gang mentality. Keep making your own decisions and don't be swayed by what others want.

Mostly Bs
You're happy to run with the pack, but sometimes you like to change your social scene, too. Sure, you understand the pressures a wolf posse can exert on a guy, but you're used to making your own decisions and mixing with a wide range of friends. A were-boy will fit into your social life no probs, and you'll mix easily with his gang.

Mostly Cs
You've never really seen the point of cliques: you think they cause more problems than they fix. And with plenty of friends with loads of different interests, you can move easily between groups. You may not quite "get" the pressures of a wolf posse, but you're tactful and easygoing enough to work around any sticky situations.

Mostly Ds

You enjoy your own company as much as (if not more than) other people's, and your wolf fella admires your independence. You're non-judgmental and will hang with all sorts, but sometimes your laid-back attitude can seem a bit aloof. Just because you don't follow the crowd doesn't mean you should turn into a recluse!

Pack Pros and Cons

Are you ever jealous of your were-guy's unconditional acceptance in his pack? Werewolves would literally die for each other, and however hairy the situation, they'll always hang in there. What could be better? Well, there are ups and downs—try putting yourself in his position.

Pack pros

* He's never alone in a pack.

* Suddenly he's got an extended family. They're the brothers he never had.

* He can get up a team for any sport you fancy, from soccer to softball.

* His packmates have advice on everything from chat-up lines to fur maintenance.

* His were-bros will help him through his first few phases, and are around to help him through any other tough times.

* The whole pack's always hungry. No one laughs when he orders thirds.

Pack cons

* He's *never* alone in a pack!

* Not everyone wants a dozen outsize shapeshifter buds in one go.

* Every night is boys' night, and sometimes he'd love mixed company.

* His packmates have an opinion on everything, whether or not he asks.

* Those sharp wolf-eyes see everything, from his first phase to his first crush, and they aren't above making wisecracks, either.

* With appetites like theirs, meals out for the gang cost a fortune!

THE VERDICT?

Did that give you a bit of perspective and help deal with your pack envy? Or do you still yearn for your own were-gang?

Hackles Up

You and your were-guy love each other's company, and he introduced you to the rest of the pack soon after you became friends. But though you've tried your best, the other guys just haven't taken to you. Even if they're not nasty to your face, you might still get a vibe, and it makes you and your boy uncomfortable. You don't want to give up the friendship, so what can you do?

Do

★ **Act nice.** Yes, it's advice that your mother would give you, but it works. Show an interest in pack affairs, read up on werewolf lore, and carry on acting polite and friendly, no matter what.

★ **Go for the girl.** She's surrounded by uber-macho oversized boys seven days a week, so any wolf-girl's always pining for some girly gossip and a chat about clothes. Leave a few of your favorite magazines scattered about next time you're visiting; she won't be able to resist.

★ **Cook!** OK, it might sound a bit 1950s, but try baking up a man-(wolf-) sized batch of cupcakes and taking them round. The best way to the heart of the pack is definitely through their stomachs.

Don't

★ **Push.** You'd love to be included, but it's not cool to shove in if the pack isn't sure about you. If you've done all that you can do, arrange to meet your were-boy away from the pack, until they come to their senses!

★ **Sound off.** If you complain to your pal about how nasty his friends are, you'll only divide his loyalties. Concentrate on the time you *can* spend together, and ignore any snubs, real or imagined. He'll be impressed by your self-control, and he may be able to talk the guys round.

★ **Get paranoid.** The reason his friends are decidedly frosty may not be anything to do with you! So don't overanalyze or try too hard. Stay natural, be yourself, and soon you'll be pick of the pack.

Making Time for Each Other

Even if your were-guy's friends are crazy about you (and particularly if they're not), every relationship needs a bit of one-on-one time. And that means you have to remind each other why you became friends in the first place. If every meeting is turning into a mass mingle, you need to find foolproof ways to escape. The trouble is, were-boys, unlike vampires, aren't psychic (at least, not with non-pack pals). Maybe he thinks you adore those rough-and-tumble outings with the boys! Don't despair.

Here's how to pick him off from his pack.

Tell him!

Werewolves aren't any more perceptive than your regular boy next door, so the first thing is to let him know that you're sick of seeing him as just a face in the crowd. Put it nicely, but make sure you're clear. It may simply never have occurred to him that you'd like to spend some time alone together.

Be proactive

If you tend to let him make the arrangements for where and how you meet, surprise him with some suggestions of your own. If they don't involve hot, crowded places, chances are that he'll fall in with your plans. Make sure he knows that you're seeing him as a friend, though. Otherwise, engineering all this "alone time" together may give him the totally wrong idea!

The great escape

What if his mates automatically assume that they're welcome to come along too? Get sneaky! Propose something no self-respecting wolf would enjoy. Offer tickets for a talk on advanced physics, for example (his friends are bound to leave you as a twosome), then grab his hand and walk out the door as soon as the slideshow starts.

And *your* friends?

If you've unloaded the wolf gang, you need to do the same with your own friends. A crowd of admiring girls cooing over your were-boy's muscles is going to be just as annoying as a bunch of huge guys showing off how super-fit they are. Maybe it's time for a little white lie. Tell your girlfriends that you're hoping for a little more than friendship with this lad (but don't forget to swear them to secrecy!). That should make them melt away like snow in the sun and leave you alone together.

Quiz: Furred Friend or Foe?

Sometimes you envy the closeness your werewolf enjoys with the other members of his pack. And at other times it seems to you that it's almost creepy how well they can read each other—they can second-guess a thought before it even comes out of your guy's mouth! Sure, they share some unusual DNA, but do they have to share everything else as well? Are you being reasonable, or is your close friendship making you a touch too possessive of your pal?

1 He's canceled *another* evening out with you, pleading "howling duties." How do you feel?
- a· OK, so long as he's rescheduled with you for tomorrow. ☆
- b· Fine. You know that with a werewolf, pack comes first. ☆
- c· Really frustrated. It's the third time this month! ☆
- d· How dare he? That's it, it's you or the pack! ☆

2 He idolizes his Alpha and keeps reciting all his "hilarious" jokes to you. What's your reaction?
- a· You find them just as witty and clever as he does. ☆
- b· Indulge him (for now); it's good he's got a role model. ☆
- c· Surely there's something a bit sad about this hero worship? ☆
- d· Storm off. This was supposed to be "you" time! ☆

3 How do you deal when your girlfriend makes snide comments about your pal and his pack?

a. Shrug them off. You know what he's really like. ☆

b. Explain why she's wrong. He's a great guy! ☆

c. Laugh along with her, but secretly think she has a point. ☆

d. Get really angry. She's really touched a nerve. ☆

4 How would you swing a run with wolves if the pack didn't approve?

a. You'd ask your friend (but let him know it's OK to say no). ☆

b. Keep dropping hints until he gives in. ☆

c. Ask him in front of his friends so he can't say no. ☆

d. Sulk. A real friend wouldn't make an issue of it. ☆

5 How does your were-boy react when his packmates poke fun at you?

a. He's furious, and phases to "settle this like wolves." ☆

b. He laughs along, but draws a line firmly under the teasing. ☆

c. He'll play along and make some jokes of his own. ☆

d. He accuses you of overreacting when you storm off. ☆

6 You discover the whole pack knows a secret you told your wolf-boy in confidence. How do you feel?

a. It's fine, you always knew about the dynamic. ☆

b. Mildly annoyed. Some of that stuff's really private. ☆

c. Cross. A secret's a secret; he had no business to share. ☆

d. Incandescent! It's a betrayal of your confidence! ☆

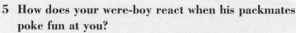

Answers: Furred Friend or Foe?

Mostly As

You always understood what the pack entailed and you're very tolerant about the limits it puts on your friendship. But you're also good at making sure that your mate understands that time spent together is important to you. You're cool, collected, and you've got a great wolf—life balance. No wonder he loves having you around.

Mostly Bs

You're a good friend to your wolf, and he's usually great at showing his appreciation. But just once you'd like to rank ahead of the pack, if only for a little while. Hints and sulking won't get you anywhere; this guy hates mind-games. Just be honest that you want to spend more time with him. Who wouldn't be flattered?

Mostly Cs

Tread carefully! If you set out to compete with this pack, you'll lose. They've got a close hold on your boy, and it's starting to worry you, but that's no reason to be a doormat. Speak up for yourself, but make sure that you don't sound like you're stamping your feet. Your wolf-boy needs to know that this is about him, not you.

Mostly Ds

Honestly, it's a surprise you're friends at all. You're naturally possessive and don't allow for the pack connection. What's more, your drama-queen tactics aren't winning over the pack. You'd be better off befriending a regular guy—one who's prepared to indulge you far, far more than a werewolf can.

Is He an Alpha?

It's not just a wolf thing! Every group has someone to look up to, admire, and obey. But being an Alpha wolf is more than just a status symbol. He's totally responsible for the pack, because keeping a bunch of teen wolves in line is a full-time job.

How can you tell whether your boy's an Alpha, or plays follow-my-leader? Look for these signs:

He gets respect

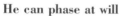

He's not the oldest or the biggest, but the other guys listen when he talks. And he expects them to. He's doesn't waste time pushing himself forward because he doesn't have to—he has their full attention, and respect, from the start.

He can phase at will

This is a huge deal for a teenage werewolf, as some have grief with uncontrolled changes for years. After all, you don't want to find yourself suddenly turning wolf in the classroom or at the skatepark! If your fella can already predict and decide when he's going furry, it's a sign that he's something special in the pack.

He makes his own decisions

Pack pressure is even more extreme than peer pressure for teen wolves—they're hard-wired to act as a group and to pay attention to what their fellow members think and feel as instinct. So a wolf guy with a strong streak of independence will likely grow up to lead the rest. Does your fella feel free to go against the pack every so often? If so, chances are he's an Alpha in the making.

He's curious about the world

Werewolves can easily be absorbed by their wolf side, all primal urges, long runs in the woods, and re-telling old legends. Future pack leaders, though, want to know as much about the world outside as they can. They're naturally curious about how they and their kind can fit into modern life. If he seems less hide-bound than his fellow packmates, he may well be an Alpha.

THE VERDICT?

Well, he may have to devote a bit more time to pack management than your average were-guy. On the plus side, you've picked the biggest, strongest, smartest wolf as your buddy. At least you can bask in the reflected glory!

Lone Wolf

You've got over any teething troubles you had with his friends and you're getting along great. You're spending lots of time together, and once or twice you've even found yourself wondering if you could be more than friends (but more on that later…). Look out! When a friendship becomes exclusive and intense, that's the point at which you risk losing your independence. Don't get so absorbed in one another that you forget your other friends and interests. Plan your time so that you can fit them in, too.

Follow these golden rules for staying an independent woman:

The night-a-week rule

This one's easy! Set one night (or day) aside for doing things you love, but he's not so keen on. Use it on anything you like and he loathes— showing off your moves on a hot, packed dance floor, or going to see one of those arty movies with subtitles that he's too impatient to read.

Keep your other friendships

Never forget that your were-guy belongs to another species. In many ways he's similar to you, but there are a few BIG differences. So spending time with your all-human friends will be a relief sometimes. OK, so maybe they're less intriguing (you already know how they work, and there's no chance that they'll morph into huge, furry carnivores however much you wind each other up!), but they're really good fun to chill out with.

Family time

Maybe it's an old-fashioned concept, but your own family are far more than just wallpaper. You've been absorbed in the dynamics of the ultra-tight werewolf relationships for a while, but don't forget about those people who are always around for you and who know you better than any of your friends—supernatural species included. Have a day or two chilling out at home to catch up on your folks' news and indulge in some good ol' fashioned family bonding.

Learn to balance

A day with the family, a day with the pack, a day with old friends... getting life on track can be a bit of a juggling act, but it's worth practicing. You've heard about the work/life balance; the were/life balance is just as important!

The Wolf Diaries III

Your friendship's turned into a bit of a rite of passage: Not only are you learning plenty about boys (and wolves), but you've picked up a whole lot of other useful stuff—how to cope with pack dynamics, for example, and how to maintain your independence while still making time for your friends. It's been a rollercoaster ride, but how are you feeling?

He's become really important to me because

....

....

....

....

....

Reasons I'm important to him, too

....

....

....

....

....

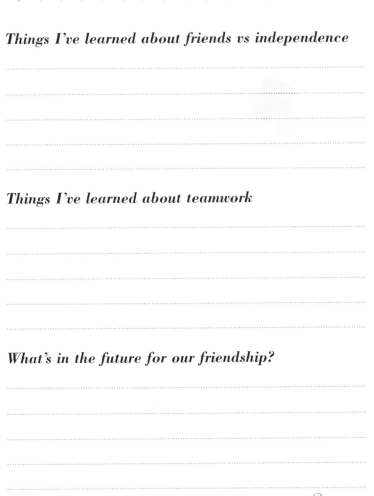

Things I've learned about friends vs independence

....

....

....

....

....

Things I've learned about teamwork

....

....

....

....

....

What's in the future for our friendship?

....

....

....

....

....

4

...But My Boyfriend's a Vampire!

You don't believe in taking the easy route, do you?
OK, so you've picked a werewolf as your best buddy
(and who could blame you? He's irresistible!), but
what happens when you've got a supernatural
sweetheart of a different species? How do you
fit in a vampire romance too?

Can you make it work with them fighting tooth
and claw? It'll test your conflict resolution tactics
to the limit, but here's how to juggle boyfriend
and best friend—without any bloodshed.

Blood Feuds

What *is* it with boys? Put a girl in between them and they get tied up about the tinest things! And if you thought human boys were bad, you ain't seen nothing yet.

Here's a guide to the biggest stumbling blocks your furry friend'll have with your undead squeeze:

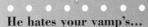

He hates your vamp's...

* Sickly-sweet scent. To you, your vamp smells of honey and sunshine; a were-guy just smells cheap perfume.

* Super-skills. Weres hate having their minds read by non-packmates. It's just not playing fair.

* His table manners. Where's the fun if you can't play with your food?

* His elegance. A vamp's unshakeable style is bound to irritate a guy who's always ripping his own clothes to shreds.

* His intellect. Your vamp's centuries of culture give a teenage wolf-boy a big inferiority complex.

Your vamp hates his...

* Wet-fur stink. To you, it's the great outdoors. To a vamp, weres smell like damp dogs.

* His speed. Vamps aren't used to being outrun. It makes them feel more prey than predator.

* His hunting habits. What he makes up for in enthusiasm, he lacks in finesse.

* His size. Vamps aren't small, but most were-boys can outgrow them by a foot or so. It shouldn't matter, but it does!

* His mechanical skills. Vamps sure can drive, but can't fix a car. Wolf-boys are a whiz with a wrench, though.

THE VERDICT?
So what *do* these two have in common? You guessed it...you!

Green-Eyed Monsters

You're head over heels for this vampire, and your werewolf couldn't be a better bud—but now your vamp's given you an ultimatum: "Him or me." Should you go along with him? No! Even if you're killer keen on your vamp, you can't let someone else call the shots on who your friends are.

If your vamp-boy's seeing red with jealousy...

Open up

Undead or alive, honesty's usually the best policy. Let your vamp know when you need some friend time. Don't keep secrets or play games; be open about who you're seeing, but make it clear it's not up for discussion. Tell him it's your night to run with the pack, and make a date with him tomorrow instead.

Stay sensitive

Yes, you need to tell your fella about your were-friend, but don't bring him up every two minutes. Just because he's a superhuman hottie doesn't mean your vamp won't get paranoid if you go on about your were-guy's hilarious quips, how much fun he is, or how much fun you always have together. When you're with your main man, stick to the here and now. Focus on the evening you're enjoying together and you'll soon convince him that he's got nothing to worry about.

Be positive

After all, you really are in awe of your vamp's superpowers—a dash of open-mouthed admiration never did any harm. There's no need to overdo it, but vamps are just as keen on flattery as any other guy. Some "oohs" and "aahs" over his flying skills or his lightning-quick reflexes will soon have him thinking that he really is pretty cool. Let him show off a little. You might be a mere mortal, but your opinion matters.

Include him

Your were-boy isn't your only friend. Try a group evening out together (put your vamp and your wolf on best behavior, and ask plenty of human buddies to come along, too). The two of them are unlikely to become best mates, but making them part of a bigger group will mean that they can mingle easily without getting on one another's nerves—or feeling they have to compete for your attention.

Green Eyed Monsters II

Take him seriously

Were-boys are faithful friends, so don't laugh him off or treat him like a kid. Listen to his worries (your vamp is too old for you, you'll get bitten, he'll get bored and fly off...), but let him know you weighed them up before your first undead date. If he's a true friend, he'll respect your judgment on the relationship.

"I really like you, but..."

This is probably not the first time a guy has had a crush on you? Of course, it's flattering, but with a vamp boyfriend and a full social schedule, you've got enough going on! If there might be a teeny romantic tinge to his jealousy, make it clear you truly value his friendship, but that's as far as it goes. Even if he's disappointed, telling it like it is will help if he's getting too possessive. And if you nip it in the bud, it's all the more likely that you'll stay pals.

Fix him up with a friend

Is your furry fella keen on you because you're the only girl he knows? After all, there aren't many were-girls he can howl to the moon with! Even if he's not your kind of creature of the night (romantically speaking), his super-toned bod and puppy-dog eyes should make him a babe magnet elsewhere, so introduce him to one or two of your bravest girlfriends. Show him off and give the other girls a chance!

Educate him!

Just the mention of the undead is usually enough to get a wolf's hackles up, however little he knows about them. Point out that he might be able to tolerate your "bloodsucker" boyfriend if he was a bit better informed, and suggest some vamp-heavy DVDs you can watch together (anything in the *Twilight* series should be a good pick—because they draw a flattering picture of were-boys as well). Keep it entertaining as well as educational —he can bring the popcorn!

Literary Love Triangles

Torn between your best friend and your boyfriend? You're not the first. Classic literature isn't just ballrooms and bodices—it's full of girls with boy-shaped heartache just like you. Read up on a few for some valuable guidance (plus it can't hurt your grades in English class!).

Romeo & Juliet

The classic doomed twosome…gorgeous teenagers falling into a red-hot affair as fate fixes their future in the darkest way you can imagine. Top choice for a romantic wallow, and if you find the Shakespearean original on the heavy side, rent Baz Luhrman's classic movie instead. It updates the story from 16th-century Italy to gangland California. Does Juliet, trapped in the wrong place at the wrong time and desperately torn between her family's favorite and the love of her life, sound familiar? Watch with tissues at the ready.

Pride & Prejudice

Maybe you thought Jane Austen was too ladylike to understand true love? Think again. Her heroine, Lizzy, is smart, sassy, and fun, but even she still manages to get a crush on the wrong guy (and fight tooth and claw with the right one) before it all unscrambles. It's a masterclass in figuring out your own feelings—and you'd do well to heed its warnings about looking before you leap. Decide for yourself which characters are most like your vamp and your wolf.

Wuthering Heights

It's a rollercoaster of a read, but what girl hasn't imagined herself as Cathy, the most romantic heroine in fiction, wooed by both the wrong and the right man? And even vamps and werewolves look wholesome and easy-to-read against dark 'n' stormy Heathcliff, the ultimate tortured hero. Great for putting your problems into perspective, this book makes your own love life look like a walk in the park!

Quiz: Friend or Foe?

Things have calmed down a bit, but your were-friend still doles out boyfriend advice by the bucketload. Does he really have your best interests at heart, or are some of his own feelings getting in the way?

1 **Your vamp takes off for a few days and it's worrying you. What does your wolf-boy tell you?**
a. To trust him...unless you've got other doubts too? ☆
b. That he's probably hunting so he can resist your scent. ☆
c. Give him the third degree! What isn't he telling you? ☆
d. That if you were *his* girlfriend, he'd never leave you out. ☆

2 **You tried getting both boys together to bond, but fur flew. What does your wolf do the next morning?**
a. Apologizes for behaving as badly as your vamp. ☆
b. Tells you to forget it; he's sorry you had a bad time. ☆
c. Blames your boy for dissing the pack all night long. ☆
d. Says you deserve better than a cranky vamp. ☆

3 How does your were-boy react if you have to cancel your plans to spend time with your boyfriend?
a. Tells you it's fine; he'd expect nothing less.
b. He's understanding and heads off with the boys instead.
c. Asks why the bloodsucker always has to come first.
d. Complains that you don't drop everything for *him*.

4 You're meeting your fanged fella's family, but what to wear? What does your wolf recommend?
a. Something flashy to show those vamp girls you've got style!
b. That you be yourself. His family will love you!
c. That you don't go at all. It's not safe.
d. His favorite outfit of yours, it brings out your eyes.

5 How does he help pick up the pieces after you and your boyfriend have had a blazing row?
a. Takes you out for a coffee and a moan about vamps.
b. Fills your day with fun to take your mind off it.
c. Threatens to tear the head off the guy who upset you.
d. Lets you have a good cry, then takes you out for dinner.

6 What would he do if you split from your vamp?
a. He'd be sorry, though maybe also sort of secretly pleased.
b. He'd be sad for you. He's not keen on vampires, but he wants you to be happy.
c. Celebrate. He's always hated *all* vampires.
d. You have a feeling he might make a move himself…

Answers: Friend or Foe?

Mostly As
He certainly *appears* to be a faithful friend, but if you look closely, there are a few sour notes. Unusually for a were-boy, this guy's a frenemy. While he's working on the best friend role (and would win an Oscar for his performance), he's also got his eye on staging a vamp/human break-up. Enjoy fun times with him, but be wary of taking relationship advice until you know his feelings better.

Mostly Bs
He's a true werewolf all the way through: honest, loyal, and 100 percent trustworthy. What a guy! He's got your best interests at heart and only wants you to be happy—even though he's not a fan of the fanged himself. Whatever happens to your love interest, hang on to this guy through thick and thin because he's the truest friend you could ever have.

Mostly Cs

Well…he's not sneaky and he's certainly fond of you, but this guy sure hates vampires. If he could split you up, he wouldn't think twice. Can you live with that? Be careful to keep him well away from your vamp and don't listen to anything he has to say about your relationship. He's too prejudiced to take on trust.

Mostly Ds

Who are you kidding? This guy loves your company and would do anything for you, but as a friend? He's desperate to date you himself! The more he hears about your undead squeeze, the harder it is for him. Is it time for a reality check about your feelings, too? You might find that you already think of him as something more…

Vamp Love: As Good As It Gets?

Being pals with a werewolf may have given you a different angle on dating a vampire. Werewolves are reliable, funny, trustworthy, and kind. Vampires, though, are…different. At first you were laid out by all that killer charm, the elegance, and the in-depth knowledge of almost every subject on earth, not to mention the supernatural powers! But is he too perfect? Are the cracks starting to show?

Is it as much fun dating a vampire as you thought?

Night owl

You're turning nocturnal! Sometimes you wonder if your vamp-boy remembers that a girl needs her beauty sleep, and it seems ages since you were awake enough during the day to spend a few hours with your girlfriends at the mall. Plus your vamp's aversion to sunshine means that your look has gone from pale 'n' interesting to just plain pale. It's not so great being kept away from all the fine weather out there.

He's a loner

Sure, he has a family of sorts, but they're not the usual kind. Being friends with a werewolf has reminded you how great it can be to be part of a big group (or a tight-knit pack), and you're finding that all that intense one-to-one vamp face time is starting to pall. There's a lot to be said for mass mingling.

He's a know-it-all

You thought all those lifetimes' experience would be fantastic when you started dating—he's done and seen it all. But it's a bit of drag when he's never, ever doing anything for the first time. And although he can (and does) keep you fully informed about…well, almost everything, you can't tell him anything he doesn't already know. Sure, it helps when it comes to homework, but it sucks in everyday life.

He's too cool for school

Or almost anywhere else. OK, maybe you started dating at the height of summer, when leaning against his—literally—cool bod helped chill you out. But you've been going out for a few months now; there's a nip in the air, and even his arm around you gives you the shivers. You'd give a lot for someone who could warm you up a little…

Gal Pal Wisdom

Your wolf-boy is your closest confidant, but sometimes you
want to chat with your own species. Your BFF was around
long before boys (vamp, werewolf, and human) showed up.

So is your gal pal up to the challenge? Tick off the traits of a true friend.

Has she always put your interests first?

Think about the past. Did she ever tell you a pair
of jeans didn't suit you because they were the last
ones in the store and she wanted them for herself?
Has she ever gossiped about you behind your
back? Or sided with the cool clique in school
against you? If the answer to every question is a
definite no, then you should be able to trust her
for true relationship advice.

Are her feet on the ground?

With a drop-dead gorgeous vamp and a larger-
than-life werewolf already competing for your
attention, advice is best served by someone
non-supernatural, to keep things in perspective.
Is your friend calm and collected enough to handle
your super-boy issues?

Would you want her love life?

Are her relationships sound and stable, or too fast to follow? What's best for a drama queen with a taste for tempestuous living might not necessarily be best for you! Plus, if she's the sensible type, with a steady squeeze of her own, she's less likely to be swayed by the sheer romance of your situation (or attracted to one of your cast-offs!).

Will she stick around?

If things go wrong in your romance, will she still be around to pick up the pieces? It's great if you know there's someone who'll be there for you, not just to help you with the difficult decisions about boys and friendship, but also to make you cups of comfort chocolate and tell you it's all going to be OK. Great as dating is—and exciting as it is to have a whole smorgasbord of tasty male talent to choose from—nothing beats a good girlfriend when the going gets tough. And be sure that she knows that you'd do the same for her, too.

THE VERDICT?

If she ticks all the boxes, it's safe to share your stresses with her, and ask her for advice. But don't forget to be there for her when she's got problems—even if hers are with merely mortal boys!

Killer Crush or Keeper?

It's amazing what a new perspective can do. Dating the undead is intense, exciting, and uber-romantic. But some regular, real-life fun with a were-boy has opened your eyes. Maybe your vamp is getting a bit too close for comfort?

Will you stay or will you go? Use our lists to help you decide:

Reasons to stick

* He really cares about me.

* I never get bored with his conversation…

* He's brought excitement into my life.

* He chose me over those gorgeous vamp-girls.

* He's really protective; he makes me feel safe.

* We look great together; all my girlfriends are jealous.

* I feel like we could be together forever.

Reasons to quit

* He doesn't like my friends.

* …but sometimes he ignores my opinions.

* Vamp "excitement" is taking over my life.

* Sometimes it's nice just to feel ordinary.

* Running with wolves has made me crave danger.

* There's more to life than image and appearance.

* But isn't forever a *really* long time?

THE VERDICT?

Did you make your mind up? Should you let him know that you want things to get a bit less serious for a while?

The Wolf Diaries IV

You've been managing the tensions between your vampire boyfriend and your wolf buddy so far, but it hasn't been easy. Ask yourself honestly whether you could give one of them up. Which one would it be? Are you ready to decide?

Is your were-boy still your best buddy?

....

....

....

....

....

Do you feel the friendship's changing at all?

....

....

....

....

....

What's happening with your human friendships?

....

....

....

....

Is your view of vampire love changing?

....

....

....

....

How are the fang—fur tensions making you feel?

....

....

....

....

PUPPY LOVE

What they say is true: A werewolf is a girl's best friend. He's seen you through the highs and lows of your vamp liaison and helped you deal with life's hurdles. He's your confidant, your pal, and your sidekick (your other mates have started to tease you about being twins...)

So is there more to it than friendship? When you're this close, might things take a romantic turn? Or have you been "just friends" for too long to see him that way? Read on to find out what your happy ever after will be...

More Than A Friend?

You and your wolf-boy have been through a lot, and stayed close even when things got chilly with your vamp chap. So would you ever go out (yes, go out in *that* way) with a werewolf? And does he see you on the dating horizon? You're no psychic, so how can you tell without actually asking?

Look out for some of these tell-tale signs:

He gets flustered

You used to be able to discuss anything with each other. But over the last few weeks he's starting to lose the plot when he talks to you, especially about your love life. The other day, you *think* you even saw him blush!

He's steering clear

OK, so he might just have a lot on his plate (and not just at dinnertime), but you think he's avoiding you. You used to spend masses of time together but now he's started making excuses whenever it looks like you'll be alone together. You haven't fallen out, so what could be wrong?

He asks how you feel

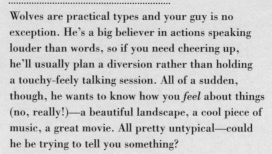

Wolves are practical types and your guy is no exception. He's a big believer in actions speaking louder than words, so if you need cheering up, he'll usually plan a diversion rather than holding a touchy-feely talking session. All of a sudden, though, he wants to know how you *feel* about things (no, really!)—a beautiful landscape, a cool piece of music, a great movie. All pretty untypical—could he be trying to tell you something?

Your girlfriends gossip

It's true that the girl who's the focus of a boy's fancy may be the last to notice. If you've been suffering worse-than-usual bouts of teasing from your friends, then it may be time to open your ears. If your girlfriends start telling you "Oooh, he really likes you!", "He left right after you did!", "He was asking if you'd broken up with (insert vamp's name here) yet", don't dismiss them straight off. They just might have a point.

THE VERDICT?

Is he showing any or all of the symptoms? If so, chances are that his feelings for you have moved beyond the merely brotherly. Perhaps it's time for you to take your own emotional temperature...

Vampire vs Werewolf

We know what they don't like about each other, but what do you love and loathe about your supernatural sweethearts? In matters of the heart, thinking clearly can be a tall order, but sometimes a good old-fashioned list works wonders!

Here are some plus points and minus marks for both to get you started:

Vamp Arm-Candy

Pros	Cons
✸ He's been around a while and can tell you a lot about the world.	✸ Sometimes it's more like talking to a granddad than a date.
✸ Forget a boy who drives …he can fly!	✸ He doesn't always say where he's flying to…
✸ He can stay calm whatever's happening.	✸ Just once it would be nice to pick a fight with him.
✸ He's independent and can take care of himself.	✸ He doesn't seem to need other people.

Wolf-Shaped Squeeze

Pros

* He's warm, both literally (he's running a toasty 108.9°) and emotionally.

* He's a real team player and loves meeting new people.

* He's completely open; you always know exactly what he's thinking.

* At heart he's just a cub. He really depends on you.

Cons

* He's hot-tempered. When he flies off the handle, he gets into a howling rage.

* He totally can't cope with being alone.

* The whole pack can tell what he's thinking and feeling—not just you!

* Under all that fur, he's easily hurt.

THE VERDICT?

Who came out on top? And when you added your own feelings to the mix, were you pleased with who won?

Quiz: How Do You Feel About Him?

You might find it hard to figure out how you feel, but are you asking yourself the right questions? To find out if your best-buddy friendship is hotting up, or your vamp-honey's charms are wearing off, take our revealing quiz.

---

1 What if your girlfriend 'fessed up to a were-crush?
a. She's your friend, he's your friend—they'd be great! ☆
b. Worried. Will he like her more than you? ☆
c. Furious, although you can't put your finger on why. ☆
d. A bit jealous. He'd make an awesome boyfriend while you're ☆
having nothing but vamp-boy trouble.

---

2 What's so great about your were-guy?
a. He's the perfect kid brother (in a very large package). ☆
b. He's cool and laid-back, *and* he's easy on the eye. ☆
c. He's gorgeous, caring, and cute, plus we've got this ☆
connection that's something really special.
d. Nothing really, you've got plenty of other friends. ☆

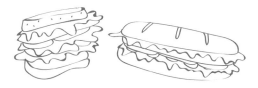

3 **Something went wrong while fixing up his bike and he's lost it. What are you thinking?**

a. Aww! A big buff guy in a little-kid tantrum's kinda cute. ☆

b. Careful! You're in too public a place to risk him phasing. ☆

c. Maybe a hug would make him feel better? ☆

d. Best to leave him alone till his buddies calm him down. ☆

4 **When he's worn out after a phasing, what do you do?**

a. Let him use your shower and make him a sandwich. ☆

b. Run off to borrow some jeans from your largest human friend—his are shredded (as usual). ☆

c. Let him know you're here for him no matter what. ☆

d. Go home to give him some space. ☆

5 **He's suggested a night out. What do you pick?**

a. Bright lights, big city! You take him at his word and drag him out to the disco. ☆

b. A night out with the pack. It's what he most enjoys. ☆

c. A walk along the river and a one-on-one chat. ☆

d. Pizza party. An cook-in where everyone's invited. ☆

6 **He's in trouble at school (again!) for flunking math. You're a math whiz, but how do you help?**

a. Let him copy your homework to get his grades up. ☆

b. Check some of his assignments before he hands them in. ☆

c. Spend some long study sessions together. ☆

d. Suggest he spends a night alone cooking the books. ☆

Answers: How Do You Feel About Him?

Mostly As

You're incredibly good friends—and it seems likely that you'll stay that way. You look out for each other, you're pretty close (most of the time you can read each other's minds), and both of you are used to taking the rough (or the furry) with the smooth when it comes to your friendship. But the warmth between you is definitely that of mates, not dates.

Mostly Bs

There's a hint of something here, but you aren't acknowledging what it might be. You certainly wouldn't be keen on anyone else dating him, though, so you need to ask yourself *exactly* why that is. Are you just a little bit worried that you'll miss the male attention? Do you just enjoy having him as part of the scenery? Or could it be that there's at least a bit of you that wants him for yourself?

Mostly Cs

Well, everyone else spotted it long ago—*you're* the only one who's being slow on the uptake. You two make a wonderful couple! Your were-boy knows it already, so how come you don't? No wonder your vamp's been acting jealous, because you're a wolf-girl at heart. Put everyone out of your misery and admit that you two belong together.

Mostly Ds

There's a spark there, sure, but you've made sure to quench it. Are you scared of your true feelings? You've hidden your heart and are playing big sis to your wolf-boy, telling yourself life's just too complicated to let him in any further. Fine, if that's how you really feel, but be sure you won't regret it if he starts dating another girl.

Why Can't I Have Both?

Love's not a crime, is it? Especially not when you're young and a long, long way away from settling down. So, since you're lucky enough to have not one but two supernatural suitors, is there anything wrong with stringing them both along?

Here are some things you might want to think about before playing the femme fatale:

Hell hath no fury

Trying to have your cake and eat it has *always* been a dangerous game, and you're playing it with boys who, between them, have far more than the regular set of sharp teeth. Forgetting feelings for a sec, what if someone gets physically hurt?

Easy way out

Maybe you like one boy better than the other, but you don't want to hurt anybody's feelings by turning them down. Think again. You risk the chance of losing both your boys if they think you're stringing them along, so do the decent thing and tell them both where they stand.

Double trouble

If you're really serious about playing them off against each other, then you don't care much about either of them. And how mean is it to toy with someone (or more than one) who really does like you? This may sound like advice from your mother, but she'd be right. Don't do it.

Don't play it safe

Do you need the security of knowing that someone's interested in you? Are you playing with your were-boy's feelings because you think your vamp's cooling off and you want at least *one* admirer? This sort of double dealing is a sign of insecurity—and if you can let it go, it's a surefire signal that you're growing up.

The best policy

Boys, whether they're undead, shapeshifters, or fully human, aren't a foreign species, not where feelings are concerned. Just like you, they want to be treated kindly, and with respect. Chances are that you can't have more than one of them entirely on your terms, so think hard about which one you really want.

What's in a Kiss?

Every song you ever listened to, every movie you ever saw, said that it's the kiss that lets you know if he's The One. As if! Kisses cause feelings you didn't know you had, sure, but it's not as simple as a happy ever after. Say, for example, you kissed your were-boy while you're still officially dating your vamp? Does it mean you have to break up? Does it mean you're cheating on him? Are you "in love"?

Here's a guide to some of the commonest kisses:

The "I really like you" kiss

This can arise out of pure friendship. You went for a walk, the moon was up, he said something endearing…it happened. Simple and straightforward. Sometimes a kiss *is* just a kiss.

The pity kiss

You know you don't have any romantic feelings towards the guy, even though he'd like you to, so you kiss him to say sorry (and it can happen the other way around, as well). Treat with caution, as it can be a recipe for disaster, particularly if bestowed on a sensitive boy who doesn't have too much experience with girls (does that sound like a wolf you know?).

The accidental kiss

We've all done it: we aimed for the cheek, we hit the mouth. And then we had to make it a "proper" kiss because we were too embarrassed not to. It's not the worst kind, but if you didn't mean it, it might be best to find a way to laugh it off sooner rather than later.

The defiant kiss

You had a row with your vamp, you went out with your wolf, and at some point in the evening he made a move. Before you knew it, you were kissing him because absolutely no one, and particularly not someone with fangs, is going to tell you what to do and who to hang out with. Proving a point isn't the best reason to lock lips, though, so it's best to own up before things get out of hand.

The romantic kiss

The kind that the songs were talking about. Your eyes meet, your lips meet, and for a moment the world stops. When this kiss happens, it's something special, so listen to what your heart's trying to tell you (if you can stop it racing, that is). Could this be love?

Just Good Friends?

One step forward, two steps back…this guy was your best friend, but now you're just fighting all the time. You thought that being truthful about how you feel should solve the situation. After all, if your warm-hearted were-boy has feelings for you that you can't return, but he still wants to stick around, it's not really your problem. Or is it?

Should you call it a day if he can't cope with being "just friends"?

Reasons to stick

* You mean too much to each other to give up now.

* He's grown much stronger and wiser from having to face the facts of your romance with a vamp.

* You're totally his closest girl-friend.

* You can't bear the thought of losing your cute were-candy escort.

* You really believe that you do him good.

Reasons to quit

* You mean so much to him it's a strain to be friends.

* Your vamp romance really stresses him out—and an unhappy were-boy is a step away from a wild wolf.

* You're getting in the way of him meeting other girls.

* You've got a vampire boyfriend whom you love more than anything.

* You did him good once, but now all you do is fight.

THE VERDICT?

Did that strike a chord? Just good friends is fine if you both feel that way—but if you don't, something's got to give.

Exit Lines

There are plenty of ways of telling a guy it's not going to work, but some of them are better (and kinder) than others. If you think you've reached the point where you need a friendship break, because he feels more for you than you can give back (for now, at least), what's the best way to let your were-boy know?

Here are 5 things to say that might soften the blow.

(1) **"It's not you, it's me."** Blame yourself. OK, maybe he's the one who tried to push the friendship into unknown territory, but there's no harm in trying to make him feel better. And it *is* you, in a way. You don't want what he wants and you can't help being irresistible (maybe keep that bit to yourself)!

(2) **"It's just a break."** Don't set a time limit, but make it clear it won't be forever. You haven't stopped being friends. If he pushes to make it a couple of weeks, or a month, or even two months, stay vague. Both of you may have moved on well within that time, but it's best just to say that you'll meet up again "when we both feel ready."

(3) **"You'll have more time with the pack."** It's worth reminding him that girl-free time can be wolf time. Even were-boys who still find their powers a little frightening can't help but enjoy running with the pack—it's like driving a sports car, but one that's within your own body. He'll miss you, but he's got blood brothers he can bond with.

(4) **"I can't be what you want me to be."** This will hurt, but it's truthful. Remind him that you two have been squabbling a lot recently; your friendship needs a rest at the very least. Saying it aloud may help him to believe it.

(5) **"See you around…"** As with any other hairy situation, don't string your goodbyes out. And keep your expressions casual. This is a good sign-off that shows there are no hard feelings.

If He Calls Time?

You didn't think it would ever happen this way round, but your wolf suggests you meet up. And when you do, he starts to tell you—really awkwardly, (he's no ultra-suave vampire, that's for sure)—that he doesn't think it can go on this way. Eventually you make out that he's trying to say goodbye.

If he's slamming on the brakes, how should you react?

Do

★ **Listen.** He's not the world's smoothest talker, and its worst liar (reassuring after those times you thought your vamp was being "economical" with the truth), so you can trust him to be honest. However upset you are, you'll feel better if you hear him out.

★ **Be nice.** Has he ever been mean to you? No. His temper may be on a hair trigger, but his heart's in the right place. Even if you've got a lump in your throat, be gracious. He's summoned up the courage to tell it like it is (and this is a boy who's terrified of girly tears), so don't throw any tantrums of your own.

★ **Take stock.** If your boy's backing out because your life is too complicated, well…you can do something about that. Make sure you've got it right: If it hit you as he spoke that he's really the right guy for you, then maybe you can clear the way for the two of you to be together.

Don't

★ **Dismiss it.** Apart from their split-second wolf phases, were-boys tend to think around a problem. Despite the super-swift wolf reaction time, he's less in touch with his feelings than you are—it's a boy thing—but he takes them seriously once he's sussed them. He's thought this through, so maybe you should too.

★ **Lead him on.** If you don't want him as a boyfriend, he's got a right to go out looking elsewhere. Don't be a dog in the manger! Admit it, he's lovely enough to have a girl of his own!

★ **Storm off.** Whether he's telling you the friendship's too uneven, he's been neglecting the pack, or he wants to get to know more girls, maybe this is something you should hear?

Fanged Farewells

When a relationship's simply run its course, it's not hard to say goodbye. But what about when one of you wants to date someone else? That can make things a bit stickier.

Here's how to part ways with your vampire boyfriend (and live to tell the tale...)

Has he guessed?

Your vamp's always cool, but lately he's been positively chilly. You're pretty sure he isn't seeing someone else—but he's a gifted mind reader, so he could have spotted that your thoughts are starting to drift wolf-wards. Before he can confront you about hiding something, it's probably time you had a chat and laid things on the line.

Have an escape route

Don't take unnecessary risks. Breaking up is hard to do, but breaking up with a vamp is downright dangerous! Let your friends know where you're going to be and have an emergency exit sorted, just in case. Allow your planned conversation half an hour—and arrange for a girlfriend to call you with something crucial that's come up if you haven't texted by then. Even if he's irritated with you, you still smell incredibly appetizing, and feeling frustrated may give him a sudden thirst.

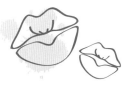

Keep it tactful

Tell the truth—but bear in mind that vamps can't abide wolves. Starry-eyed descriptions of your romantic moment of truth will go down very badly. You want to survive to enjoy the dating game, so don't wind him up. Simply say that your feelings are very confused right now and you want him to feel free to find the girl he deserves.

Keep it short

When you're nervous, it's natural to run on a bit. Don't. Have your speech ready, deliver it as calmly as you can, listen to what he has to say—then leave. Spinning things out won't make either of you feel better. Fond reminiscences of the happy times you've had together can wait until time has taken the edge off, and you're ready to meet as friends.

Returns Policy

Yes, you DO have to give his gifts back! That ring your mom thought was a fake, the valuable first edition of "Wuthering Heights", the fabulous pendant with the really large ruby...all of it. Sorry, but if you're breaking up, it's the least you can do. Even if they're hard to part with, in the long run it'll give you closure.

New Dawn

You've been friends for ages, so how do you start to be...something else? It may feel funny at first, but you've been dating with an open mind for a while, so it shouldn't take long to adjust. After all, plenty of girls wouldn't date a vampire...but you did, and you've lived to tell the tale (there may even be a book deal in it some day...).

How will dating a werewolf be different?

He's straightforward

Vamps are gorgeous, but even their number one fans would admit they can be hard to read. If you've got used to it, dating your wolf will come as a shock—he means what he says and he says what he means. If you've learned to play games in a relationship, relax. You don't need to with this boy.

He's warm

You can abandon all those extra scarves and sweaters you needed while dating your below-zero vamp and break out the T-shirts. Your were-boy was always good for defrosting chilly hands; now that you're entitled to get up close, he can keep you toasty all over.

He's a pack player

It was sometimes an issue when you were just friends, too: This guy is the opposite of a loner. He loves to go out with the gang, and now you're his girlfriend you'd better get used to it. The more the merrier will always be this guy's motto, but if you learn to love the pack (and let's face it, they're pretty great), then it won't get on your nerves.

He's a boy's boy

He loves to fix things, he's super-keen on sports, and he isn't always terribly good at explaining his feelings (or even understanding them). And he knows absolutely nothing about art movies or Japanese prints. In fact, he's far, far more like a teenage human than your vamp ever was. Your cultural interests may have to be indulged with like-minded girlfriends from now on.

You're equals

Admit it. When you were dating a vampire, he sometimes made you feel pretty young. He was an old soul in an incredibly cute teenage bod, after all. Your werewolf can certainly compete on the physical front (you've lucked-in in the looks department), but he's a teenager, just like you. Prepare to fight, make up, and generally date on a level playing field in comparison. He may be a werewolf, but you'll be surprised by how similar you really are.

The Wolf Diaries V

Whew! When they said the path of true love never did run smooth, they weren't kidding. But whether things hotted up or cooled off with your were-boy, how do you feel about the way it turned out? And what's next?

Would I have done anything differently?

....

....

....

....

Do I feel I've lost a friend?

....

....

....

....

Any regrets?

Are we in it for the long term?

How I feel

Index

Index